Washington Wizards

Richard Rambeck

CREATIVE EDUCATION

Published by Creative Education
123 South Broad Street, Mankato, Minnesota 56001
Creative Education is an imprint of The Creative Company

Designed by Rita Marshall

Photos by: Associated Press/Wide World Photos, Focus on Sports, NBA Photos, UPI/Corbis-Bettmann, and SportsChrome.

Photo page 1: Chris Webber
Photo title page: Rod Strickland

Copyright © 1998 Creative Education.
International copyrights reserved in all countries.
No part of this book may be reproduced in any form without written permission from the publisher.
Printed in the United States of America.

Library of Congress Cataloging-in-Publication Data

Rambeck, Richard.
Washington Wizards / Richard Rambeck.
p. cm. — (NBA today)
Summary: Describes the background and history of the Washington Wizards pro basketball team, formerly called the Bullets, to 1997.
ISBN 0-88682-892-9

1. Washington Wizards (Basketball team)—History—Juvenile literature.
[1. Washington Wizards (Basketball team)—History. 2. Basketball—History.]
I. Title. II. Series: NBA today (Mankato, Minn.)

GV885.52.W37R36 1997   96-52960
796.323'64'09753—dc21

First edition

5 4 3 2 1

Other cities in the United States have more people than Washington, D.C. Other cities have more trade and business activities. But no American city is as important to the day-to-day operations of the country as Washington, D.C., the nation's capital. Washington is headquarters for most of the important offices of the federal government. It is where the president lives, and where federal laws are made and judged. It is home to such famous landmarks as the Capitol, the White House, the Washington Monument, the Lincoln Memorial, the Jefferson Memorial, and the Vietnam Veteran's Memorial.

Washington is not located in one of the 50 states. It is in

All-time Bullets great Kevin Porter.

1 9 6 2

Walt Bellamy's 2,495 points and 1,500 rebounds as a rookie Packer are still club records.

the District of Columbia, which is what D.C. stands for. Actually, Washington is the District of Columbia, because the city's boundaries and the district's boundaries are the same. The city is located on the Potomac River between the states of Maryland and Virginia. It has been the national capital since June 10, 1800.

Washington is best known for its political activity, but it is also a city with a rich sports history. The National Football League's Washington Redskins are part of that history, along with the Washington Wizards, the city's National Basketball Association (NBA) franchise. Like the nation's capital, which was originally located in Philadelphia, the Wizards didn't start out in Washington. But the team has enjoyed its best days in the shadows of some of the most famous landmarks in the United States, and behind such talented players as Chris Webber, Juwan Howard, and Rod Strickland, they hope to bring a championship to the D.C. faithful.

THE PACKERS DON'T PRODUCE VICTORIES

The Washington franchise began in 1961 as the Chicago Packers, an expansion team that was added to the NBA's Western Division. The club managed only 18 victories during the 1961–62 season, but rookie center Walt Bellamy performed remarkably well. He averaged 31 points and 19 rebounds a game, and was named NBA Rookie of the Year. A year later, the team had a new name, the Zephyrs, and a new young star. Sharpshooting first-year guard Terry Dischinger tossed in 20 points a game and became the franchise's second consecutive NBA Rookie of the Year winner.

Power forward Harvey Grant.

Abe Pollin and two partners purchased the Bullets for a then-record price of $1.1 million.

Dischinger and Bellamy gave the team hopes of a bright future, but that future wouldn't be in Chicago. The Zephyrs' home court, the Chicago Coliseum, wasn't big enough. In addition, the owners felt that Chicago fans had never really taken to the team. The club moved to Baltimore for the 1963–64 season and became the Bullets.

The team did improve in its new hometown, making the playoffs after the 1964–65 season. In the playoffs, the Bullets upset the St. Louis Hawks in the first round before losing to the Los Angeles Lakers in the division finals. Two years later, however, the Bullets returned to their losing ways, finishing with a 20–61 record.

THE PEARL SHINES IN BALTIMORE

The team had three coaches during the losing 1966–67 season, the third of whom was Gene Shue. Although he knew it would be a big repair job, Shue was determined to pick up the pieces of the team and put them together to build a winner. One of the major components of Shue's new club—a 6-foot-3 guard from little Winston-Salem College in North Carolina—was selected by the Bullets in the 1967 college draft. The backcourt star's full name was Vernon Earl Monroe, but his friends called him the "Pearl." He would prove to be a gem for the Bullets.

Monroe had been a breathtaking star in college. In his senior year, he averaged more than 40 points a game. Despite Monroe's great ability to score, some pro scouts weren't sold on him. One scout said the Pearl relied "too heavily on razzle-dazzle stuff." Another reported that "Monroe dribbles in circles and between his legs, shoots off balance, and makes like a whirling dervish. It works for him at the small college level, but [I] doubt he can pull it off with [the] NBA schedule."

Even the Bullets had their doubts about Monroe, but they drafted him anyway, hoping their gamble would pay off. It did. The Pearl quickly took control of his game and became the NBA Rookie of the Year in 1967–68. He averaged 24.3 points a game, dazzling opponents and Baltimore fans alike. "That Monroe is unbelievable," said New York Knicks guard Walt Frazier after one game. "I don't think the Pearl saw the basket on some of his shots, but he's that kind of shooter."

The Baltimore players believed Monroe could take the team to the championship level. "Earl is the superstar we've been needing to compete with the other strong teams," explained Bullets guard Kevin Loughery. "Don't be surprised if he leads the league in scoring. It's not that I think we're a one-man club. It's just that, in clutch situations, it's only natural that we look for Earl to take charge, to get the basket we need. If you need a big hoop in the last seconds, the best thing to do is clear a side for him."

Guard Kevin Loughery led the Bullets with 356 assists for the year.

UNSELD GIVES THE BULLETS INSIDE MUSCLE

The Bullets needed more than Monroe's heroics to become a great team—they also needed muscle under the boards. They needed a guy to grab rebounds and get the ball to the Pearl, an unselfish player who would do the dirty work while Monroe, Loughery, and forward Jack Marin poured in the points. The Bullets got all of this when they

Wes Unseld, a Bullets star.

SHETTLER LIBRARY

The legendary Earl "The Pearl" Monroe.

drafted Westley Unseld, a 6-foot-7, 245-pound block of granite from the University of Louisville.

Led by Unseld and Monroe, the Bullets posted the best record in the Eastern Conference during the 1968–69 season. Monroe averaged 25.8 points a game and was named first-team All-NBA. But it was Unseld who really brought the Bullets together. He became only the second player ever to be named both Rookie of the Year and Most Valuable Player in the same season. Unseld didn't score a lot of points, but he did everything else in a big way. "Unseld was the big difference," Atlanta Hawks coach Richie Guerin reasoned. "They [the Bullets] were losers before, and they're winners now. And Unseld is the only change they made."

Unseld was the shortest center in the NBA, but he used his size and incredible strength to muscle his way in for key

1 9 6 9

Gene Shue shared in the Bullets' postseason honors by being named NBA Coach of the Year.

MVP and Rookie of the Year Wes Unseld.

rebounds. Once he was in position under the boards, he was almost impossible to move. Unseld might have been a first-year player, but he didn't play like a rookie. "Actually," said Bullets coach Gene Shue, "it's hard to regard him as a rookie. He does the job of a player who's been in the league for years." It was a job that some fans didn't even notice, because Unseld wasn't flashy. "It's not my job to look good," he explained. "It's my job to make other people look good."

Unseld's teammates appreciated his efforts to help them out. "Wes is just beautiful," said Bullets forward Ray Scott. "The other team shoots, Wes goes for the ball, and the rest of us go charging downcourt. He hits one of our guards at midcourt with one of those two-handed, over-the-head passes of his, and somebody else winds up with an easy layup."

The Bullets made winning look easy during the 1969–70 season. They advanced all the way to the Eastern Conference championship series against the New York Knicks. After losing the first two games of the series, the Bullets rallied behind Unseld in game three. In that game, the big center grabbed an amazing 34 rebounds. What made that total almost unbelievable was that the Knicks as a team had only 30 rebounds. "It was a great effort on his part," said Knicks center Willis Reed, who guarded Unseld all night. "I've never seen one man outrebound a team before—in the pros, in college, or on the playgrounds."

Unseld and Reed battled through seven tough games. The Knicks finally won the hard-fought series four games to three. New York then went on to claim its first NBA title. The following season, the Bullets won the first of three straight Central Division championships. Baltimore made it all the

1 9 7 0

Backcourt star Earl Monroe averaged a team-leading 23.4 points per game.

way to the 1970–71 NBA finals, but were stopped cold by Milwaukee in a four-game sweep. The Bullets were disappointed, but they knew they had the type of team that could bring home a championship.

ON THE MOVE

Unfortunately, it would take eight years before the Bullets could claim that elusive NBA crown. By then, the club would have a new home and many new cast members. Team management still believed it could build a top-caliber team around Unseld, but decided that changes needed to be made in other positions. Monroe was traded in 1972 to the New York Knicks, whom he helped lead to the 1972–73 NBA title. The Bullets, meanwhile, got power forward Elvin Hayes in a trade with the Houston Rockets.

The Bullets were making a lot of moves on the court, and they also were making moves off the court. The team constructed a new arena in Landover, Maryland, which was on the outskirts of Washington, D.C. Bullets officials decided to change the name of the team to the Capital Bullets so that fans in Washington would think of the team as their own. But that idea didn't work, and the club soon became known as the Washington Bullets.

The Washington Bullets had little trouble drawing fans, and one of the reasons was Elvin Hayes. Known as "The Big E," Hayes was one of the top talents in the league. He had been branded a loser in Houston, however, because he couldn't turn the Rockets into a successful franchise all by himself. Many Houston fans blamed Hayes for their team's failures.

Jack Marin set a club record in free-throw accuracy (.894) in his last season as a Bullet.

A Bullets trademark: tough defense.

The one and only Elvin Hayes.

When the Bullets traded for Hayes, coach Gene Shue told his new star not to worry about what the fans expected. "Nobody is going to blame you if we lose," Shue told Hayes. "Nobody is going to say anything if you miss a shot or commit a turnover. Just play ball, Elvin. Forget all that stuff you got in Houston. All that is over."

Shue's advice worked; Hayes looked happy and relaxed on the court in Landover. "The Big E has been a gem since the day he arrived," Shue claimed. "I mean a G-E-M. He has worked very hard. I couldn't be more pleased."

The Bullets won the Central Division title in 1973–74. A year later, Washington claimed another division title. This time the team made it all the way to the NBA championship series for the second time in franchise history.

Phil Chenier's 2.29 average steals per game set a Bullets all-time record.

Washington was expected to roll right over the underdog Golden State Warriors in the finals. Unfortunately, the Bullets shot nothing but blanks against the Warriors. Golden State shocked the experts and the rest of the NBA by sweeping the series in four games. The Warriors, who had only Rick Barry as a big-name star, won by playing better as a team than the Bullets. Washington learned from Golden State's example, and began building its own close-knit unit over the next two seasons.

The Bullets brought in Dick Motta as coach. They also traded for small forward Bobby Dandridge, a quicksilver player who could explode for a ton of points in a hurry. Dandridge, Hayes, and Unseld gave Washington probably the best front line in the NBA. Reserve forwards Mitch Kupchak and Greg Ballard provided valuable contributions off the bench. The backcourt was solid but unspectacular.

Chris Webber, a star of the 1990s (pages 18–19).

First-year Bullet Tom Henderson led the team with an average of 6.9 assists per game.

Kevin Grevey, Charles Johnson, and Larry Wright were all streaky but effective shooters.

The Bullets were not dominant during the 1977–78 regular season, finishing with a so-so 44–38 record. But Dick Motta's players went into postseason play confident that they had the chemistry of a champion. Washington defeated Atlanta in the first round, San Antonio in the second round, and Philadelphia in the Eastern Conference Finals. Then the Bullets advanced to the league championship series, where they faced the Seattle SuperSonics.

Seattle won two of the first three games, forcing the Bullets into a must-win situation in game four. The game was played in Seattle's Kingdome in front of almost 40,000 screaming fans. Although the Bullets fell behind by as many as 15 points in the second half, Unseld, Dandridge, and

Sharpshooting guard Dave Bing.

Hayes keyed a late rally that gave Washington a 120–116 victory. Seattle then won game five, but the fired-up Bullets rolled to a 117–82 victory in game six to even the series.

The Bullets journeyed to Seattle confident that they would bring back their first NBA title. After a close first half, Washington started to pull away early in the third quarter. The Sonics were concentrating on stopping Elvin Hayes, which opened up scoring opportunities for Unseld, Ballard, and Grevey. Then, in the fourth period, Seattle mounted a comeback, cutting the margin to five points with a little more than one minute to play.

Bob Dandridge was the Bullets' leader in steals with 101.

The Sonics worked the ball around for a good shot. Guard Dennis Johnson drove to the basket but lost the ball, producing a wild scramble. As bodies hit the floor, the ball rolled right to Washington's Mitch Kupchak. The Seattle fans groaned as Kupchak cleared the ball to Grevey.

With Washington in possession, the Sonics were forced to foul to try to get back in the game. It didn't work. The Bullets made their free throws, and Wes Unseld grabbed two critical rebounds in the last minute to preserve the lead. Washington won the game 105–99, and Unseld was named Most Valuable Player of the series.

The Bullets returned home to a wild celebration in the nation's capital. The city was relishing its first major sports title since the Washington Redskins won the National Football League championship in 1942. The Bullets' celebration included a parade down Pennsylvania Avenue and a visit to that avenue's most famous building, the White House.

"Bruise Brother" Jeff Ruland.

WASHINGTON WINDS DOWN IN THE 1980S

Bullets fans came close to celebrating another championship the following year. Washington posted the best record in the NBA during the regular season, then advanced to the league title series. The opponent, again, was Seattle. Washington took game one at home, but the SuperSonics rallied to win the next four contests and claim the title. The Bullets' stay atop the NBA heap was over. The team had gotten old, and Dick Motta knew it would take an overhaul to make the Bullets a championship contender again.

Motta left the team, as did Unseld, who retired, and Hayes, who was traded. Former Bullets coach Gene Shue was named the head man again. He built a solid team around center Jeff Ruland and forward Rick Mahorn, a pair known as the "Bruise Brothers." The Bullets made the playoffs after the 1981–82 season, but then fell into a slump.

The franchise made several key changes in the next few years. Washington traded for Cleveland forward Cliff Robinson, and then got high-scoring guard Gus Williams from Seattle. In 1985, the Bullets added sharp-shooting guard Jeff Malone and 7-foot-6 center Manute Bol. Malone averaged 22 points a game during 1985–86, and Bol led the league in blocked shots. But the team still posted a losing season, its fifth in the last seven years. Shue was fired and replaced by Kevin Loughery, a former Bullets player.

Loughery's team immediately got a boost when center Moses Malone signed with the Bullets as a free agent in 1986. Malone had led the Philadelphia 76ers to the NBA title in 1983, and Loughery believed he could do the same for

Elvin Hayes ended his Bullets career as the all-time leader in points, field goals, free throws, and blocked shots.

Washington. The center carried the Bullets into the playoffs in both of his two seasons with the team, but Washington lost in the first round each time.

Manute Bol stood tall in blocking 15 shots during a game against the Atlanta Hawks.

KING CROWNS AN ALL-STAR COMEBACK

The Bullets never really got back on track under Loughery. The coach was fired in the middle of the 1987–88 season and replaced by Bullets hero Wes Unseld. Unseld's work was cut out for him because Moses Malone had left Washington, signing as a free agent with Atlanta before the 1988–89 season. As a result, the new coach needed to begin rebuilding the team almost from scratch. In seeking someone to be the cornerstone of the "new" Bullets, Unseld turned to forward Bernard King, a player trying to rebuild his career. King had been one of the top scorers in the NBA during the early 1980s when he played for the New York Knicks. But his career seemed over after he suffered a horrible knee injury in 1985.

King tried to make a comeback with the Knicks. That didn't work out, but when he moved to the Bullets, he immediately became one of the team's top scorers, averaging 20.7 points a game in 1988–89 and 22.4 points a game in 1989–90. But King wanted more—he wanted to be among the best in the league again. Experts said his bad knee wouldn't allow him to reach that goal, but King proved them wrong.

The Bullets forward led the league in scoring during the first half of the 1990–91 season, averaging more than 30 points a game. In a couple of games, he even scored more than 50 points. Bernard King was all the way back, and he knew it. "To come back after the entire knee was reconstructed," King said. "To come back from seeing 40 metal staples running down the middle of my knee. To come back from being unable to lift my leg off the bed without help from my physical therapist. To come back from a surgery performed to allow me to walk properly again. To come back and get 50 points in a ball game again is one of the most special feelings in the world. It's something I will never forget. And it's something that I'm awfully proud of."

King's pride was boosted even more when he was selected to play in the 1991 All-Star Game. Unfortunately, the Bullets couldn't match King's success on the court during the 1990–91 season. Despite the solid play of King, guard Darrell Walker, and forward Harvey Grant, Washington had one of the worst records in the league. That meant it was time for more changes and more rebuilding.

Versatile Bernard King ranked second in the club for points, rebounds, and assists.

HOWARD AND WEBBER REUNITED IN WASHINGTON

During the early 1990s, the Bullets tried to win with a mix of veterans and youngsters. Through trades, they acquired center Pervis Ellison and shooting guard Michael Adams. They acquired Tom Gugliotta, Calbert Chaney, and 7-foot-7 Gheorghe Muresan of Romania through the draft. While the Bullets were setting franchise records for attendance, their record only got worse. In 1993–94, the Bullets were 24–58, last place in the Atlantic Division. But Muresan developed more quickly than expected. He became a key part of the major rebuilding that took place before the 1995–96 season, when Jim Lynam was chosen to replace

Forward Juwan Howard, an all-around star (pages 26–27).

Before being traded, Michael Adams led the Bullets with 6.9 assists per game.

Wes Unseld as head coach. But the biggest news of that off-season wasn't about the new head coach—it was the reunion of former college teammates Juwan Howard and Chris Webber, who joined Muresan in the Bullets' frontcourt.

In college at the University of Michigan, Howard and Webber had been part of a team of five fabulous freshman known as the "Fab Five." In two years, the Fab Five made it to the NCAA Finals twice. The second time, in 1993, Michigan had a good opportunity to beat North Carolina, but the team saw their opportunity vanish when Webber called a time-out late in the game. Since Michigan had no time-outs left, Webber was called for a technical foul. North Carolina made the penalty shots and went on to win.

That was the last time Michigan's Fab Five played together, as Webber announced he was leaving college for the NBA. Webber, drafted by the Orlando Magic, was traded on draft day to the Golden State Warriors. He was the first sophomore since Magic Johnson to be selected first overall in the draft, and he went on to become NBA's youngest-ever Rookie of the Year. But because of friction with Golden State coach Don Nelson, he asked to be traded after his first year.

Meanwhile, Juwan Howard, the Bullets' first-round draft pick, had been holding out. In a bold move, the Bullets gave up Gugliotta and future draft picks in a trade for Webber, and with his old college chum on board, Howard had all the reason in the world to sign a Bullets contract.

At Michigan, Webber had been the flamboyant team leader, and Howard was the solid man in the background. When the two were reunited with the Bullets, an injury to Webber's shoulder kept him from returning to the level of play he had shown during his rookie year. The Bullets won only 21 games in Webber and Howard's first year together. When Howard took on the role of leader, and Webber was relegated to the background, people wondered if the reversed roles would strain their friendship.

Howard responded to the rumors: "Despite what people say about it being his team or my team, we look at this as being two leaders who set the tone for the rest of the guys."

Webber echoed Howard: "We're closer now than when we were at Michigan—100 percent closer—and we were so close at Michigan, it was scary. Now it's time for us to win. That's all that matters now."

And winning is exactly what the Bullets began to do. With Howard, Webber, and Muresan, the Bullets finished 39–43 in 1995–96. Despite Webber's continued problems with his shoulder, that was an 18-game improvement over the previous year. Howard scored 22.1 points and pulled down 8.8 rebounds per game. Muresan was named the NBA's Most Improved Player, averaging 14.5 points and 9.6 rebounds per game.

Then, prior to the 1996–97 season, the Bullets added veteran point guard Rod Strickland. He quickly became the team leader in assists, and overcame his reputation as a troublemaker. Webber returned to the lineup full-time following shoulder surgery to prove that his rookie season hadn't been a fluke.

"With a talent like Chris Webber and a point guard with Rod's experience, I look forward to that combination," said coach Lynam of the Bullets' future. "If you look at our team as a whole," Lynam continued, "you have a lot of young,

After a year-long absence, Brent Price sank an NBA-record 13 consecutive three-point shots.

The high-scoring, high-profile Chris Webber.

Gheorghe Muresan, a giant force under the boards.

Rod Strickland was one of the NBA's top five players in assists per game.

athletic, talented, big people and to plant an experienced guard like Rod with them, I think that is a huge plus."

In 1997–98, the Bullets' name changed to the Wizards, and they moved into a new home, the MCI Center. There's little doubt that Washington fans will continue to fill the franchise's new home, and the team would like nothing more than to earn such dedication by bringing an NBA championship home for their fans. "My expectation is that this is a playoff team and then some," said Lynam. And while Lynam may be right about Washington's future, he won't be in the picture. In early 1997, Lynam was replaced by Bernie Bickerstaff, a former Bullets player who had spent the previous seven years in Denver, serving for a time as both general manager and head coach. As a Bullets player from 1973–85, Bickerstaff was a pivotal member of a team that made the playoffs 10 times, the NBA finals three times, and won a championship in 1978.

As Washington's head coach, Bickerstaff emphasized defensive play and solid execution. "He has tried to give us a structure and a little bit of discipline," said a rejuvenated Strickland. "He told us where he wants guys to be when certain things happen. I think that we have a better understanding of where we're supposed to be."

Bickerstaff believed in his team and wasn't afraid to tell them so. "I have no problems with this team's effort. I am convinced they are a team that wants to win," the head coach said. "I think the chemistry is there, we just have to find it." The excitement of a new head coach and a few more victories on the scoreboard should give the Washington faithful a lot to hope for in the future.